Mama Vo's Bánh Xèo

Hardcover ISBN: 979-8-9854379-1-1
Paperback ISBN: 979-8-9854379-0-4

facebook.com/mamvosbanhxeo

Mama Vo's Bánh Xèo

Glossary

Bánh xèo (BUN say-oh):
sizzling pancake. It has a savory taste and is filled with shrimp, pork slices, mung beans, and bean sprouts.

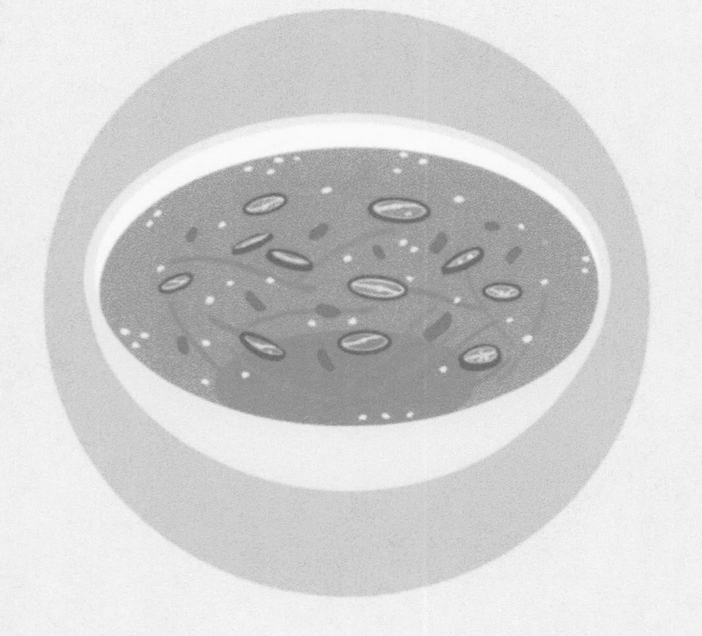

Nước mắm (NOOK mum):
fish sauce. It is a sweet, savory, and spicy (if you want!) dipping sauce. This is common in countries like Vietnam, Thailand, and the Philippines.

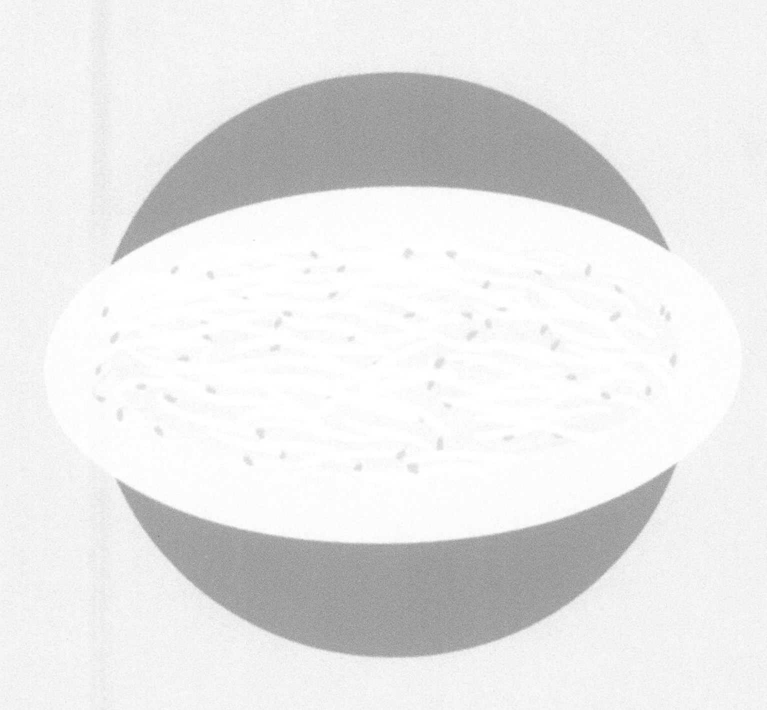

Bean sprouts:
a type of vegetable used in many Asian countries.

Lucky red envelope:
it contains money to wish children luck and prosperity on their birthdays or for the Lunar New Year. This is popular in countries like China, Vietnam, and in other parts of Asia.

"Good morning!" Max greeted his stuffed animals. He picked up his favorite turtle and whispered, "Good morning, Max."

"Guess what day it is today. It's my 8th birthday!" Max dressed in his favorite outfit and ran downstairs.

福
9
1 2 3 4
5 6 7 8 9 10 11
12 13 14 15 16 17 18
19 20 21 22 23 24 25
26 27 28 29 30

SIZZLE! POP! HISS!

"Mmmm. That smells so good," Max said.

"Happy birthday, honey," his mom said as she handed him a lucky red envelope. "I made your favorite food to take to school."

"Bun say—oh!" Max said with a smile. He stuffed the red envelope into his pocket.

"That's right," his mom said. She flipped the golden rice flour made like a pancake. It made a loud, snappy sound.

SIZZLE. POP. HISS.

Max took a big whiff. “I can’t wait to eat it!”

Mom packed the bánh xèo into his lunch box. She also added a small plastic container filled with sauce. "Every bánh xèo needs…" she began.

"Nook mum!" Max agreed. "Like how every pancake needs syrup!"

"Yes, and I made the nước mắm just the way you like it," said Mom.

Max sprinted through the front door to catch the bus. He could not wait to tell his classmates all about his lunch.

During morning share, Ms. Carpenter asked Max what he was most excited about for his birthday.

"My special lunch!" Max exclaimed. "It's called bánh xèo! It has shrimp, pork, and bean sprouts. You wrap it with some lettuce and then dip it into nước mắm. Every bánh xèo needs nước mắm like how every pancake needs syrup."

All his classmates wore blank looks on their faces.

"It sounds delicious, Max," Ms. Carpenter said as she moved the class into their math lesson.

Max plodded back to his seat and slumped into his chair. As the other kids took out their notebooks and filled in today's math sheet, Max picked at the skin on his arm.

"No one understands me," he thought.

When lunchtime finally arrived, Max found an empty seat in the cafeteria. He opened his lunchbox, pulled out his chopsticks, and lifted the lid of his small plastic container.

"What's that smell?" Caleb said to Hunter.

"It smells like fish mixed with stinky socks. Gross!" Hunter said and pinched his nose.

"I don't think I can eat my own lunch now," said Caleb. He scooted all the way to the other side of the cafeteria bench.

Max's face turned red like his lucky red envelope.

He no longer felt like eating his special lunch. Instead, he threw the lunch into a garbage can.

While his classmates ate their turkey sandwiches and laughed, Max ate nothing at all. He buried his head in his arms.

Then, someone sat down beside him. It was the lunch lady! She held a familiar food in her hands.

Max's eyes widened. "You eat bánh xèo, too?!" he exclaimed.

"Bánh xèo was my favorite meal when I was a little girl. My mom, Mama Vo, made it for me all the time. She even passed down the family recipe," the lunch lady said. She split her bánh xèo in half.

Max held out his hand for the piece of Mama Vo's bánh xèo. "That looks so good. Did Mama Vo teach you how to make it?"

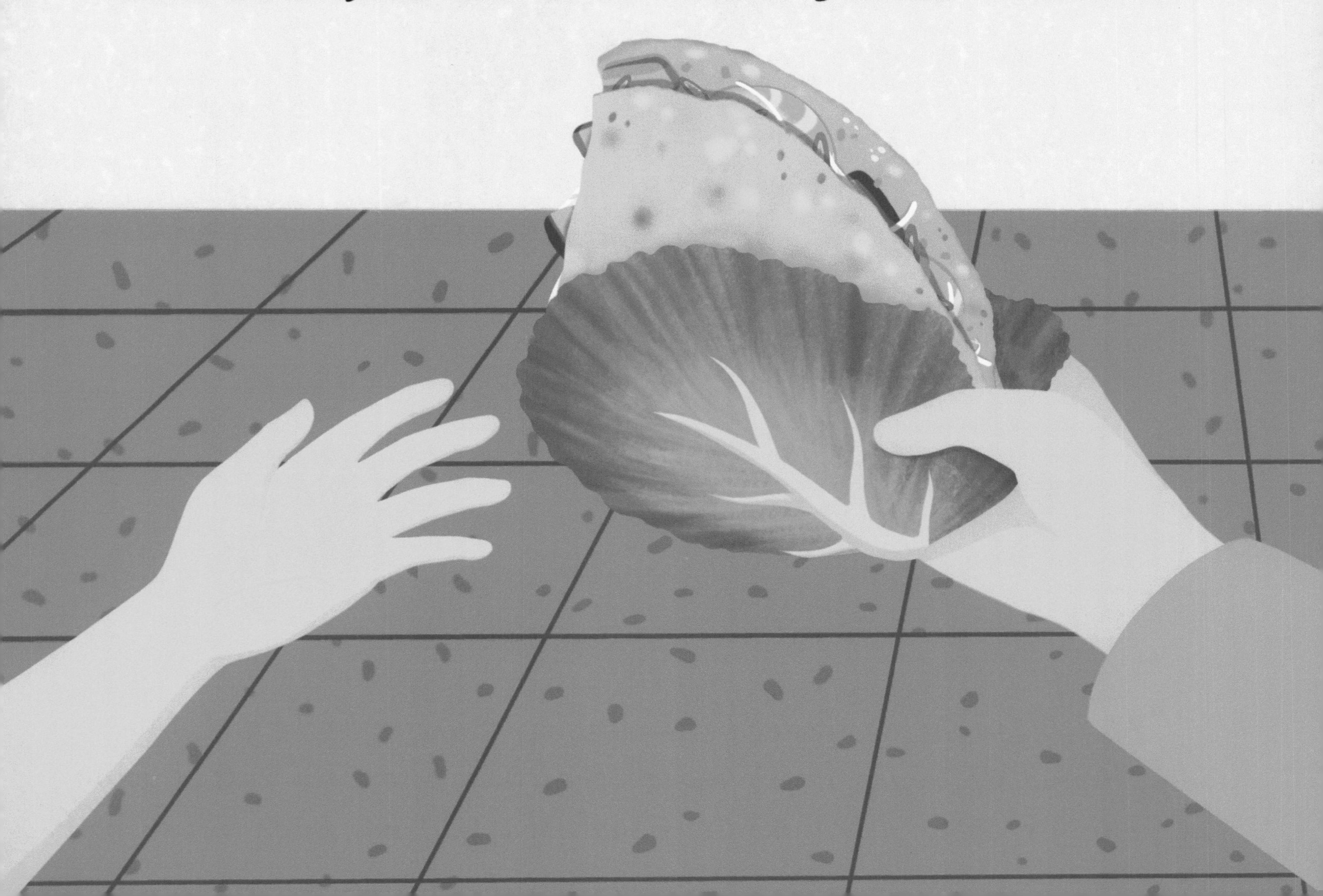

"She sure did. But she added chili peppers to hers because it gave her mouth a kick." The lunch lady laughed. "I bet she loves that I'm sharing it with you."

"Sometimes, other people won't understand you. They don't know what bánh xèo and nước mắm are because they've never had them. They might say mean things about your lunch or about you.

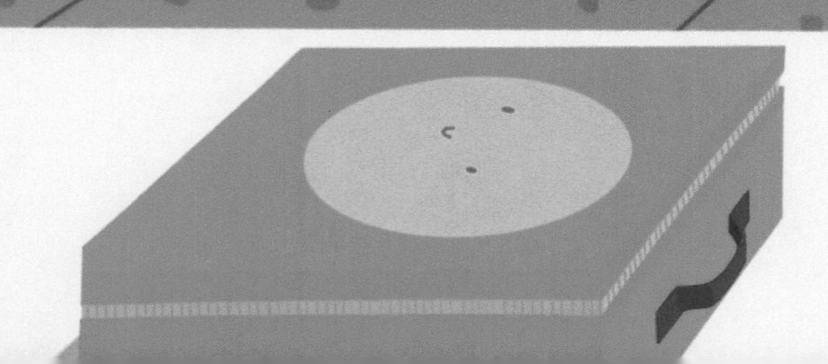

But you're the only one who can
choose how you want to react.
Now, don't forget the nước mắm,"
she reminded him.

"Of course. Every bánh xèo needs nước mắm like how every pancake needs syrup," Max grinned.

"You know why bánh xèo is a very special meal? Because it's a part of your culture and identity as a Vietnamese-American. Your mom and grandma, and even her grandma, all ate bánh xèo before you."

"Even Mama Vo's grandma ate bánh xèo?" Max chimed in.

"Yep. Food is a part of who you are. You should appreciate it every chance you get."

Max looked at the garbage can. "I won't throw it away next time," he said.

As they finished their last bites of Mama Vo's bánh xèo, Ms. Carpenter's class was called outside for recess.

"Thank you for the bánh xèo," said Max

"You are most certainly welcome. Mama Vo will be proud that you now know the importance of bánh xèo."

Before Max left the cafeteria, he opened the lucky red envelope from his pocket. Behind the crisp dollar bills from Mom, he found a note that said:

Enjoy the bánh xèo,

no matter what others think!

Max knew the 8th was a birthday he would never forget.

About the Author:

Fiona Tsang is an elementary school teacher in New York City. She received her Bachelor of Arts in childhood education and dance from CUNY Hunter College. Fiona loves to tell stories about Asian-Americans through words and movement. She is thrilled to share her first published book with the world!
You can find more information at facebook.com/mamavosbanhxeo and on Instagram @mamavosbanhxeo!

About the Illustrator:

Victoria Tang is an illustrator based in Brooklyn, New York. She graduated with a BFA in Illustration at School of Visual Arts. Her works range from traditional to digital mediums, focusing on narrative storytelling and characters through her pieces. For her portfolio and more information, go to facebook.com/mamavosbanhxeo and check out her work on Instagram @smilieperson!

CPSIA information can be obtained
at www.ICGtesting.com
Printed in the USA
LVHW021606180522
719024LV00008B/235